VISSARION

ALSO BY T. G. AYER

Young Adult Paranormal

THE VALKYRIE SERIES

Dead Radiance

Dead Radiance Audio

Dead Embers

Dead Embers Audio

Dead Chaos

Dead Chaos Audio

Dead Wrath

Dead Silence

Joshua - Dead Radiance

Joshua II - Dead Embers

Joshua III - Dead Chaos

Joshua IV - Dead Wrath

Joshua V - Dead Silence

THE HAND OF KALI SERIES

Fire & Shadow

Blood & Gold

Time & Fate

Fury & Virtue

Spirit & Soul

THE DARKWORLD ORIGINS

Pyros (Logan)

Ailuros (Kailin)

～

THE DARK SIGHT SERIES

Dark Sight

Cursed Sight

Vissarion

Shadow Sight

Dark Prophecy

Cursed Prophecy

Shadow Prophecy

～

THE APSARA CHRONICLES

Immortal Bound

Gods Ascendent

Dominion Falling

Vengeance Born

Last Legion

～

A SEASON OF ASH AND BONE

Heartfyre

～

Adult Sci-Fi

HANDS ASSASSIN

Death Dealer
Death Mark
Death Strike
Hand's Assassins Series

∾

NEW ADULT CONTEMPORARY THRILLER W/A TONI VALLAN

Beautiful Collision
Beautiful Conviction

∾

PSYCHOLOGICAL HORROR W/A TONI VALLAN

Dark Shadows
Splinter

VISSARION

A DARK SIGHT NOVEL #2.5

Cover art by Eduardo Priego

Cover art © T.G. Ayer. All rights reserved.

ISBN-13: 978-0995112612

ISBN-10: 0995112614

 INFINITE INK BOOKS

VISSARION

USA TODAY BESTSELLING AUTHOR

T.G. AYER

CHAPTER 1

The problem with wishing that life would change, that things were different, was that some things you wish come true and it's nothing like what you'd hope for.

At fourteen, Maximus Vissarion had made pushing boundaries and bending rules into a serious art. His parents owned a vineyard in the hills of Ralabia State, and lived a comfortable life, and as such, were completely at a loss as to how to deal with his rebellion.

For Max, rules confined him, suffocated his spirit. Or perhaps, that was just a nice way of couching the truth—that he was ungrateful and uncontrollable.

Chores were…a chore, and almost anything set him off. His upbringing meant he'd grown to be a little arrogant and was far too stubborn and unbending. School was hours spent in a restrictive hell, and the only thing he enjoyed about it was the sport. Wrestling fit well into his spirit, the need to burn off energy with the added advantage of violence was a thrill he tended to live for.

He'd often entertained dreams of entering the Olympics—before they'd suggested that full nudity would return as the dress code.

Max had laughed at the thought, though he'd felt a ripple of discomfort at the prospect and had shied away from opportunities offered by the larger entertainment consortiums who also headhunted young wrestling stars.

Men in Max's time were not known for being shy, but Max had been raised with a strong sense of self-respect. Perhaps some would deem it as a negative, that he'd rebel against everything his parents taught him, or expected of him, though he chose to retain a strong hold on his respect for this body.

"Max, you're just a prude, just admit it," Augie teased, his eyes scrunched up in his round face so much that they appeared as mere slits above rounded cheeks.

Julius and Eduard both laughed and nodded, eyes watching Max for a response. They were sitting at the edge of the bath, resting after doing their lengths for the day.

"Or maybe you're just shy," said Julius, a glint in his eye that Max was sure was more malicious than the boy himself would have admitted.

Max shook his head and smiled, keeping his tone even and pleasant. He'd found that when in an argument, an even, calm tone won sooner than yelling or words spoken in anger. "You do realize I've had no problem strutting my stuff in the locker rooms, or even at the beach, clothed or unclothed. But the one thing I refuse to do, is to put my body on display in auditoriums all around the world in the name of a sporting event which benefits only the governments and councils as opposed to the actual participants."

"Look at you, becoming all libertarian and shit," said Eduard, grinning despite the hard response. "Have you forgotten all the money you are missing out on?"

Max shrugged. "Do I look like I need the money?" Max pushed off the edge of the water and stood to his full height. "If anything, I have a duty to leave those positions to people who need the money. Although, it depends on how much of the winnings those players actually pocket. We all know their sponsors dip into the winnings and take their cuts way before the player even sees a dollar."

Augie's eyes widened. "You really swallowed that bullshit?"

Max reached for a towel from the bench behind him and began to dry himself off. "I could ask you the same thing. Have you swallowed the propaganda that the government is selling? Aren't we supposed to live in a world where freedom of speech has value?"

"Yeah. As long as you're not an Apollo disciple," Julius muttered, his eyes darkening.

The group of boys fell silent. Though the time of the worldwide persecution of Apollo worshippers had long passed, the period of horror still lived on in the proof they saw every time they passed an Apollo temple.

The building remains broken, columns toppled and crushed, statues destroyed.

Max took a deep breath. "Yeah. Look at what happened when people stood up for what they believed in." He sighed, tired now of a conversation that had gone from heated to one that made him feel ill.

Not that he'd have admitted in public, but Max and his family had long been disciples of Apollo's word. And even though a century had gone since their forefather's lives had been torn asunder, his people still looked over their shoulders, still studied the expressions of friends, neighbors, and coworkers, looking for the telltale signs of someone who would betray them.

It was an illogical thing, and yet it had perpetrated through generations, and for some reason, Max held onto it to remind himself that courage under adversity was of far more value than following the government's words as though they were handed down by the gods.

"Come on. This conversation is depressing. Let's go and get something to drink." Max was already halfway to the locker rooms as he called out to his friends over his shoulder, "Last one to get dressed is buying."

Spurred by the challenge, the three boys surged from the water and hit the locker room, dragging clothing onto wet bodies and grunting as they shoved each other aside to get out the door.

They reached the street in an indecipherable knot of elbows shoved into ribs and feet attempting to kick the legs out from under their other friends.

A near collision with a young couple pushing a stroller was enough for the four to straighten and calm themselves, but it was only a few seconds before they were off again, striding as fast as they could across the street toward the local coffee bar, the Black Roast.

Max had meant to overtake his friends, head past the shop and hightail it home, because coffee was the last thing he wanted. Coffee made him sleepy, and he quite liked the little high that he usually rode on.

He'd gotten almost all the way past the Black Roast and was looking over his shoulder as the three boys following him when things seemed to slow down, as if time had paused.

The three boys stared, hands moving slowly to point in his direction. He sensed the person beside him, and was already turning, but even as he spun around, he knew there was no way he'd avoid the collision.

He crashed into the woman, a part of his brain aware that her frame was slight, her bones thin, and as she bounced off him, he reached for her. He caught her hands just in time, grateful that she'd grasped him as hard as he had her, or she'd have fallen backward onto the stone path.

Miraculously, time returned to normal, and Max found himself firm on his feet, enough to steady the old woman too. He smiled apologetically and paused to help her to her seat.

Wide, bright blue eyes stared up at him from a wrinkled face, and she smiled cheerily up at him, the expression incongruous given that he'd been expecting her to slap him hard or call for the police.

He waited only long enough to lower her into the seat before stalking off following the trio of friends who he'd now labeled as traitors. They'd left him to deal with the old woman and had hurried off. He shook his head, jogging to catch up with them, vowing he'd not let a single one of them win at handball.

They'd been playing for almost an hour when Julius had cocked his chin at something beyond Max's shoulder.

"You have an admirer, Vissarion." Julius smirked, and Max threw the ball at him a little too hard. He ignored the 'oof' his friend emitted as the hard leather-covered ball hit him full in the gut.

The old lady now sat on a bench across the path on the other side of the court.

CHAPTER 2

The playground was large, dotted with climbing gyms and exercise equipment, a range of activities for all ages.

All forms of seating were available from fallen logs to concrete steps to grassy knolls and benches. The woman he'd almost knocked to her death—she certainly looked fragile enough to have broken had she hit the ground too hard—now sat quietly on the bench, her hands folded in her lap as she people-watched.

Frowning, Max turned back to the boys and continued to play, determined to ignore her. Despite the boys' teasing that he'd acquired a groupie, Max ignored the woman for a while and then, in the space of a few minutes, decided what he was doing wasn't right.

Gasping for breath, he threw the ball to Augie and said, "I'm going to go see what she wants. Who knows, she probably wants to arrest me or something."

"What if she does?"

"So be it. I'll say my piece. You guys will speak for me, right?"

All three assured Max they would, and he left them to cross the court and head toward the bench.

Here goes nothing.

As his feet drew him toward the woman, he resolved that should she proposition him, he'd turn her down politely. It wasn't unheard of for younger men to take older women as lovers, and he didn't have anything against people who would choose such a lifestyle. Only, it wasn't something he'd ever considered, so if that was what the old woman as after, she'd be sorely disappointed.

Besides, what else could she want from him? Max was frowning as he paused when he reached the stone path. He hesitated there for a moment, oddly enough. He'd walked over with every intention to speak to her and now that he was a few feet from her, he found himself unable to move.

She tilted her head and studied him with her bright blue eyes. Her hair was gray and piled up on the top of her head, half up and the rest hanging at her back in soft curls. She was petite, and appeared fragile enough that a stiff breeze would likely knock her over.

She waved him over, and he found his feet obeying even though he'd all but decided he wanted to turn and run back to his friends. Perhaps this was a mistake, and he hadn't thought it through.

What if the woman was looking for a slave? Perhaps she was part of a human slave ring, stealing young boys and selling them off to rich sheiks in a far-off desert.

Then she let out a soft breath and patted the bench beside her. "Sit, my dear boy. Please sit. We have much to talk about."

Laughter bubbled up from inside him. *They* had much to talk about? What was this old woman on about? He didn't know her apart from almost toppling her over. But, out of respect drummed into him by his parents, he swallowed the laughter and schooled his features.

She leaned against the bench, the sunlight reflecting off her pale hair, and he saw a beauty in her, one that told him she must have been a stunner in her younger days.

Now she smiled serenely. "Young man, you are so much more important than you know," she said, her voice shaking, confirming her advanced age.

Max swallowed and remained silent, partly because he wasn't sure what to say to that, and partly because he was still contemplating running for his life.

Then she smiled, and Max understood that his silence had pleased her.

Strange old bat.

"You are a rare breed my boy. And I mean that literally." She leaned toward him, and he had to steel himself against bending away. She met his gaze and asked, "Do you know how important you are?"

Max could only shrug in response. What kind of a question was that? He felt like he was in some kind of herb-induced dream. Maybe he'd wake up soon and find it was all a figment of his imagination.

"One day you will come to work with me," the old woman said, her smile growing wider. "You are the one. I touched you . . ."

Uh oh.

Max was beginning to be convinced that the woman was a little *touched*, perhaps senile considering her advanced age.

"I knew you'd be here. A dream…it was a dream that brought me here and I knew the moment I touched you." She paused to stare at his face. "It's the touch, young man. The touch…it's what tells the truth of it all."

A little unnerved and a lot uncomfortable, Max got to his feet. Possibly all that talk of touching him had gotten under his skin. He was beginning to bet a little heavier that she was a slave trader.

"Don't go. I think I've scared you," she said reaching out. She stopped short of touching him when she saw the look in his eyes.

Max shook his head. "I'm not scared."

Liar.

CHAPTER 3

"*P*ssht. It's good to be scared," the old woman said, letting out a cackling laugh. "Keeps the blood in your veins warm."

Again, Max was at a loss for words. The old woman set his nerves on edge for so many reasons, but oddly, he didn't find himself running for the hills. Something about her assured him that despite her oddness she was safe enough.

So far, he'd acted out of instinct, catching her in time before she fell, coming over to speak to her, not running off before she said her piece. Still, though he was waiting to hear what she really had to say, not the nonsense about touching. If she continued on that vein, he'd be gone in an instant.

"You must have heard of the prophecies, of the destinies of the oracles. They search for these women, decade after decade, century after century. They put them through tests, make them jump through hoops, all because of a tweak in their DNA, the curse of a bloodline." The old woman sighed and rubbed her palms together. She ran her fingers over the back of her hands, and it was easy for Max to see how pale and wrinkled her skin was, how papery thin it was.

She seemed to be absently wiping something off her left hand just above the fingers, then she turned her palms over and stared at them. He wasn't sure if she was reading her lifelines or if she was imagining seeing something covering her skin.

Max sat there and let her talk softly, wondering not for the first time what in Hades' name he was doing sitting with her. She was definitely senile.

Max's lip curled. He didn't need to be here. He was popular, he knew people, important people. He had a future ahead of him. Sitting here with this old woman was so out of character for him.

And what would people think if they saw him? He glanced up and scanned the empty court. His friends had left him, possibly to head straight to tell the rest of their classmates what a weirdo he was.

This little stunt, his moment of community service, would probably be his downfall.

"You think you're special, don't you?" she asked, her words pulling him out of his thoughts. When he met her gaze, he found himself staring at her blue eyes, now flashing with what he interpreted as criticism.

"I...er..." Stammering just made him furious. Max hated feeling uncomfortable.

Then she laughed softly. "Well, you are special. Just not in the way you expected. Or probably not even in the way you want."

The old woman's blue eyes sparkled although her smile was sly. She seemed to enjoy directing their conversation, as if she liked him being in the dark as she fed him bits and pieces of information.

Well, she may enjoy it, but Max certainly wasn't about to put up with it.

He shifted in place, projecting an air of confidence—that he didn't have—and folded his arms. "Special how?" he asked. His muscles were taut, his jaw tight as anger filtered through him. But that anger was edged with curiosity. She may have said a lot of things that he'd have to chalk up to senility, but what fourteen-year-old in his right mind didn't like to know he was special?

"You are Immunis," she said, her voice swaying with music, her eyes joyful. In her exuberance, her voice broke, and she took a breath, looking away beyond Max's shoulder.

But he was no longer paying attention to her state of mind. Her words had piqued his curiosity. Forehead scrunching, he asked, "What's an Immunis?" He leaned toward her. "What's so special about it?"

Immunis.

The sound of the word sent a thrill through his blood, but perhaps it was just because he'd never heard it before. Was this part of her seduction? He was still yet to find out what it was that she wanted from him.

She didn't answer the question. Instead, she met his curious gaze, her blue eyes, a little cloudy now, briefly became clearer. "You are unique. In all the world, there is only one of you. And you are vital to me and to my kind."

"Your kind?"

Worry skittered down Max's spine.

What was her kind? Was she one of those creatures from outer space, from one of those planets one saw when using those gigantic telescopes at the observatory?

Then Max stiffened. What if she was one of the Gifted. Over the last century or two, people from all walks of life had slowly begun to reveal the powers they possessed.

Or better yet, she could just be on some kind of black market drug for the elderly.

Or she really could just be senile as he'd thought to begin with.

He started when she spoke again, bringing him out of his thoughts. "Do you know what an oracle is?"

Of course, he did. He was tempted to tell her that, but instead, he merely nodded.

"What about a Pythia?"

Max couldn't help himself. He rolled his eyes and bit back a frustrated sigh. "If you don't know about the Pythia you may as well be dead." He looked at the old woman for a long moment. She'd spoken confidently, making him wonder. "Do *you* know the Pythia?"

She smiled then, her eyes sparkling. "Perhaps I ought to have introduced myself." She shifted until she faced him, then extended her hand to him. "My name is Aurelia Julian."

Max felt his mouth fall open and for once he didn't care how that would look. *"You're* the Pythia?"

CHAPTER 4

She gave a short nod, and her expression clouded, as if her happiness had fled with the mere reminder of who and what she was. Then Max frowned, glancing around the park. "But shouldn't you have security? Like bodyguards or protection?"

"Why?"

"Because if people knew who you were when you walk by them on the street, they wouldn't leave you alone." He scanned the area around them again, this time looking for anyone who seemed to want to listen to their conversation. But he and the oracle were alone.

He sank back against the backrest, relieved. "Don't you care that they'd find out?"

The oracle shook her head. "Not at all. They don't see me. I'm old and unimpressive. Most people will walk straight past me."

Max opened his mouth to reply, but then he paused. He'd been about to object, to assure her that it wasn't true. But then he realized there was a kernel of truth in her claim. Hadn't he only stopped because he'd bumped her and he wanted to make sure she didn't fall and get hurt on his account? If he hadn't knocked her over he'd likely not have seen her at all.

And he suspected that even if he'd bumped into her, he'd have waved a vague apology and continued on his way.

When he looked over at her again, he found that she was grinning at him. "It's understandable. It is what I prefer. The anonymity is refreshing. I can move amongst the people without being disturbed. I've spent so many years in my life serving them, they've forgotten I am still human, just like them." She sighed and sat back, her expression serene as if it didn't bother her that people ignored her existence. He wasn't sure what to make of it.

Even so, he still had to wonder what it all had to do with him. She still hadn't properly explained what she wanted with him. Perhaps he wasn't all that good at hiding his thoughts because Aurelia reached out and patted the back of his hand, the movement comforting.

"Very well. I will no longer keep you in suspense." Her smile widened, and she settled against the back of the bench and folded her arms over her narrow chest. "Do you know how the oracles see?"

Nodding, Max replied, "You touch a person, and then you can see their future." He kept this tone even despite the worry that kept flickering in his mind; his parents would be looking for him. Joachim Vissarion was not the most patient of men, and the horses probably needed to be watered and fed soon.

Aurelia smiled. "Yes. It's why I try not to touch people even if by accident."

"Why not?" Max frowned.

"Because there is the issue of privacy. Some people do not want to know what their future holds. Most people will only come to me if there is a good reason. There is only a certain type of person who wants a window into their future."

Max found himself understanding her more than he'd expected to. He himself, despite the desire for success, for achieving his goals in life, even surpassing them, he'd never been of the frame of mind to speak to a seer about his future. "I think I know what you mean. Those who have something to gain by it."

"Very good. You catch on fast."

Then Max did a double take, the blood in his veins chilling. "But I touched you. When I bumped into you." He stared at the old woman, his eyes wide with shock. "Did you see my future?"

Happiness shone from Aurelia's eyes as she stared at him, shaking her head in what he thought was disbelief. And, of course, joy. Which to Max was really strange. "I didn't," she replied softly. "And that is why you and I are here having this talk."

"Because you didn't see my future when you touched me?" The old woman was too confusing. Usually, Max would never admit to being befuddled by anything—it was too great a blow to his young ego to admit ignorance of any sort—but in this case that's exactly what he was. Confused.

The old woman sighed and shuffled to the edge of the bench. Then she stood and carefully straightened, and Max was certain he'd heard a few of her bones creak.

"That is what it means to be Immunis. You are immune to the Seer's touch." She turned to look at him, a serene smile spreading on her lips. "You, my dear boy, are destined to be the Voice of the Pythia."

Max boosted to his feet, a rush of fear rippling along his limbs. The old woman's words were insanity. Yes, people knew about the Pythia, even feared her ability. But nobody that he knew of ever aspired to the position of her Voice. In fact, he'd never even heard it was a real thing. Just whispers from a past filled with myths and folktales.

"I thought they were just a myth."

"A myth as much as the Pythia?" Aurelia asked, smirking as she straightened to stare up at him. Again, he was struck by how small and fragile she was. He didn't regret coming here to help her, to look out for her. But things had taken a turn for the weird.

"So, what is it you want from me?" he asked. Strange how well he'd taken her revelation. It's entirely possible that he'd lost his own marbles as well.

The old woman didn't reply. Instead, she reached out a hand and waited, and Max could only assume she wanted him to offer her his arm.

He did.

She seemed pleased as she tucked her hand into the crook of his elbow. "Walk me to my car, young man. We need to make arrangements for your training. And I will need to speak to your parents."

Max was taken aback by Aurelia's suggestion, but didn't object as he walked her to the edge of the park to find an ancient Ford chugging away as it awaited her return. The taciturn driver got out to open the door for the old woman, and she pulled Max inside the car and bade him close the door.

Max gave the driver his address and remained silent as they drove through the hills toward his family's vineyard. Aurelia had fallen oddly silent, and Max had been reluctant to disturb her in case she was taking an old lady nap or something.

When the driver drew up in front of the Vissarion Vineyard's main house, Max alighted and helped Aurelia to exit the vehicle. By the time the old woman had righted herself and faced the door, Max found his parents both standing there, a little confused.

Neither appeared angry though, which Max counted as a win.

Aurelia walked up the stairs and paused before Joachim and Kassandra Vissarion, and introduced herself, her voice hushed as Max climbed the stairs.

Both his parents turned to stare at him as he came to stand beside her. In response, he lifted one shoulder and raised both his eyebrows. This was none of his doing, and he wasn't going to hesitate to defend himself.

Aurelia was invited inside and welcomed to the dinner table where she inquired after Max in such detail that he began to feel uncomfortable. Grades, sporting actives, friends, attitude to elders and even his performance around the vineyard.

Why would she want to know such details?

Still, Max's parents had answered her as best they could while casting sidelong stares at Max when he clamped his mouth shut in defiance. He still wasn't sure he'd want this—whatever it was—to go any further.

His mom had wanted a further explanation as to what the Immunis was, and how Max was expected to fulfill such duties. And that was when Vissarion senior had used his legendary negotiation skills. He'd gone in, passionately demanding that Max receive at least his basic military education while working for Aurelia.

To his father's surprise, Aurelia had happily assured him that the training involved in strengthening his standing as an Immunis would easily surpass that of any military academy in the country.

Not long afterward, Max had been shipped off to Aurelia's remote estate in the hills of Argentina.

CHAPTER 5

Max's feet slammed into the solid ground as he ran, sweat beading on his neck and dripping along his shoulders and down his spine. He felt the vibrations of the impact with the earth run through his limbs, through his bones. He ran bare-chested, though he'd refused to ascribe to full Spartan-style nudity.

Over the months, many of the women in Aurelia's camp had expressed interest in Max, and he'd turned them all down. He'd grown in the last two years, taller, more muscular, drawing more attention from both sexes. He suspected that much of that interest was purely admiration as opposed to serious consideration. Or so he'd hoped.

Only a small handful of the women who worked on the estate, and of those engaged in warrior training, were near his age, and yet even the younger women hadn't appealed to Max. Not that he'd been immune to their beauty. He did have eyes in his head after all.

What with all the training in the hot Argentinean sunshine, he often encountered women, their thin cotton training shifts soaked with perspiration to the point of being transparent.

Still, even the sight of luscious breasts of varying shapes and sizes hadn't elicited more than a passing self-admission of admiration.

Now, as he ran in the hills, half hidden by the dense over-growth of greenery, Max considered what his life had been thus far, and where it was going, and whether he'd made the correct choice.

Max had stepped off the helicopter all those months ago, more convinced than ever that a military career was what he aspired to. He'd been amped up, intending to demand Aurelia arrange an interview with the NGS army for him and request an early entrance. But he'd arrived and been received by a man who appeared to be of military stock.

General Codimus had welcomed him with a terse announce-ment that Max would be training under him for the duration of his summer break. Though Aurelia had requested Max be removed from formal schooling, his parents had refused, although the elder Vissarion had implied he'd reconsider if Max gained early entry to the army.

Apparently, Max had inherited his stubbornness from his father.

There had been a point when Max had considered that his training was far too tiresome considering it spanned all of his summer holidays, not to mention long weekends off being trained at a local army facility.

But the one surprising factor of his edification where it applied to the Oracle Aurelia was language. He'd learned the ancient tongues of Latin and Greek now, and spoke them all fluently with Aurelia.

As interesting and different as things had been, sixteen-year-old Max found it hard to adjust to a life without his friends. Although the first six months had gone with him being chop-pered back and forth for training in Argentina and then long periods of locally based training, he'd begun to miss his friends and to question if he really did want to spend his life translating visions for an old woman who'd already managed decades without him.

She'd often talked of the destruction of the Pythia line, of people who lurked in the shadows waiting for the moment to strike. Max had chalked that up to an old woman's ravings, but a part of him had wondered if perhaps he had an obligation to ensure she remained safe.

But then he'd question why him. What made him, in particular, the best person for the job?

Max had been so focused on running, on the rhythm of his breath and the burn in his muscles that he'd almost missed the sound of a set of hoof-beats, thundering on the ground and growing ever closer.

Slowing to a stop, Max stared around him, unsure of the origin of the sounds, unable to pinpoint the direction in which the rapid hoof-beats were moving. Was he in danger? Or was he just being paranoid?

The hoof beats drew closer, and the leaves on the trees shuddered, the pebbles and loose soil on the ground raised with each vibration.

Max whirred around, the perspiration on his skin cooling as fear struck deep.

A gigantic beast tore through the trees, and it seemed as though time slowed.

The beast pawed the ground, steam spurting from his great nostrils. Red eyes glared at Max, and his heart stilled. The beast lowered its head, and despite everything he'd been taught Max took a step back. His instinct told him to run, as fast and as far as he could.

But the step away seemed to enrage the beast even further. It lurched closer, horns dangerously close to Max's face. It seemed as though time refused to pass, making that one moment last forever.

Finally, Max's heart began to thrum again, and he took a slow long breath. If this was his moment to die, then so be it, but he wasn't going to run. It really made no difference. In the choice between being gored facing his killer or being mauled while running away, Max chose to look the beast in the eye.

CHAPTER 6

The giant boar let out a soft roar and stomped closer, its glistening snout stopping an inch from Max's bare chest. The monster had lowered its head, and the metal ring through its nose glinted in the sunlight.

Max froze.

A gold ring?

Was this beast domesticated?

It seemed unlikely, especially considering how dangerous the beast appeared to be. Max exhaled slowly, forcing his breathing to take on an even rhythm.

He kept his eyes lowered, head down, waiting as the creature huffed and sniffed him again. Max was unable to calm his rapid heartbeat and decided that it didn't matter any longer. If the beast had been of the mind to maul him, he'd have done it by now.

Or so Max hoped.

When the boar tossed its head, Max glanced up and found himself sucking in a shocked breath as he stared into a pair of eyes that were not...eyes. They were obsidian orbs filled with living flame, flickering and shimmering and yet seeming to *see* Max.

Now that he was looking at the boar instead of hiding his face as though he were prey, Max was stunned to see the creature's body shimmer, as if the edges were fading into another dimension. Blue sparks of electricity flickered along the beast's skin, emphasizing that this was no ordinary creature.

The boar tipped its head and sniffed Max again, this time its nostrils grazing Max's chin.

Well then.

It appeared the creature wasn't about to maul Max to death.

So, Max decided that perhaps he ought to make friends. He lifted a hand and reached out to lay his palm up the beast's neck. But instead of submitting to Max's offer of friendship the boar growled and reared back, snorting loudly before shook its head.

And then he disappeared.

Perplexed, Max stared at the empty spot where the beast had stood only a second ago, wondering if he'd imagined the whole thing. But a stray thought teased at the back of his head. The boar meant something, or it was here to tell him something.

Then Max shook his head and stared around the clearing, not sure what he was searching for. Perhaps to find someone lurking waiting in the shadows, laughing at the trick they'd played on him. Which was entirely too illogical.

Max backed away and walked slowly through the trees. His heart still raced, but he'd accepted that he'd seen something. But he wasn't yet sure what it was.

Continuing his run, Max followed the route back to the estates, studying the trees as he went. When he reached the main house, he hurried up the stairs, something still disturbing his mind. Not that the sight of a gigantic living breathing fire-eyed magical boar was not disturbing enough.

Inside the main hall where Aurelia took her meetings with her liaisons from around the world, Max found himself drawn to the murals on the walls. It seemed his subconscious knew more than he did, because it didn't take him long to find what he was looking for.

The murals were painted floor to ceiling, the images were life-size, or close enough that they seemed almost real. Images of Pythias from across the ages, sitting beside fires, hands raised, expressions intense. Here and there were images of a Pythia alone, but not alone.

In nearly almost every painting, was a smoky image of a human-sized boar.

With a golden ring in its nose.

Max was staring up at the boar, unsure how he felt about having dreamed up a meeting with the boar, considering it was an element in the mural. Had his subconscious remembered seeing it during all those months that he'd been coming to the hall.

"I do believe you've met Xales," said a voice from Max's side.

He turned to Aurelia who beamed at him, her faded teeth shining with glee.

"Who?" asked Max although his gut was telling him the truth.

She pointed at the boar. "Xales. He's the Pythia's familiar. He follows the Pythian line, guarding the presiding oracle during her time in her role as seer for humanity."

Max grunted. "What does that have to do with me?" he asked, still half unsure that Xales was real.

Aurelia snickered. "Denial will not help you today, young man. From the look of you, I can see you've stared into the eyes of the beast. And the fact that you are still alive attests to who you are."

Max scowled. He disliked when the woman talked in riddles

But Aurelia just chuckled. "Xales is tasked with guarding the pythia and also with the protection of the Immunis to a certain extent."

Max had to force his mouth closed.

A magical boar was going to protect him in case he was in danger.

Could things get any more crazy than that?

CHAPTER 7

*A*t the age of sixteen, and before shipping off to army training, Max had spent one last summer at the estate in Argentina.

And his last visit there had ended on a surprising note.

Two years had passed that had seen Max training under Aurelia's various tutors. His lifestyle had been rigorous and stressful, and he'd worked harder than he'd ever thought himself capable. But he'd begun to wonder why.

He was Immunis, and connected to the line of the Pythia's by virtue of his ability to repel their sight, but he'd still not been told what it meant in the greater scheme of things. Max had spent the last two years learning to interpret Aurelia's prophecies, growing to understand the nuances of the old woman's expression.

Her foretellings were done in Latin, and sometimes in Ancient Greek, and she'd taught him to remember every word, and to guide her with the correct questions. It hadn't taken long before he'd sat beside her when the representatives of the New Germanic States Army visited.

The contingent was led by a man of impressive bearing, a Commander Cornelius Aulus who had walked into the reception room of Aurelia's manor, his presence seeming to dominate the entire hall. Mara, Aurelia's handmaiden, who was most definitely no maiden, and absolutely not a servant, had apprised Max of who and what Aulus was.

A rising star in the NGS army, Aulus had been selected as a representative to the Pythia on behalf of the NGS government. He'd come with the stamp of approval of the NGS senate and the president.

Max had stood off to one side, watching the man with trepidation.

"Are you afraid of him?" asked Mara with a bland smile. Her gray eyes sparkled as she watched his face, as if his reaction was of great importance.

Max hesitated. He was tempted to deny his fear, but then he thought better of it. A man without fear is a reckless man. And Max intended to never be reckless. So he sighed and said, "Yes. I am. His bearing, the power in his body language…even if I didn't know who he was or who he worked for, it would be easy to understand that he is a man who commands power."

"He's moving up in the ranks. Well-respected across all the world senates and governing boards." Mara sighed. "He's descended from the Moorish slaves, of Ethiopian stock to hear him tell it. And, though not many know this, his maternal line can be traced back to a Pythia from the tenth century."

Now *that* had surprised Max. "So the representatives to the Pythia must bear her genetic stock? Or is it merely an advantage to be of the lineage."

Mara smiled and shook her head. "Merely an advantage. Although I must admit that it seems strange that a man of his standing would want to be the delegate to the Pythia." Then the old woman chuckled. "I want to be in the room when she tells him."

"Tells him what?" Max asked.

But he didn't get an answer. Instead, Mara grabbed his ear

and shuffled off, pulling him along with her. Max's sharp "Ow, that hurts," was thankfully muffled by the rise in conversation as the delegation was let through to meet Aurelia.

Max tugged his ear free and rubbed it, scowling at Mara who just beckoned him closer. Clearly, according to the old hand-maiden, he wasn't too old to have his ear pinched. He followed closely and wound his way between the gathered contingent who were being shown to small stone benches arranged in an oval.

Aurelia had a flair for the dramatic, but Max was of the opinion that she'd already done so much for the world that she deserved some of her eccentricities. Mara directed Max to stand at Aurelia's right-hand side while she positioned herself at the oracle's left. Commander Aulus was being led to his position at the first bench on Aurelia's left, and Max wondered at how Mara had allocated him so he could see Aulus's face clearly.

Later he would understand why.

CHAPTER 8

*M*ara called the meeting to order in her shaky, croaky voice and Max had to hide a smile. She handed the meeting over to Aurelia who tipped her head at Aulus. "Welcome to my humble home, Commander Aulus. And I extend my welcome to your *contingent.*" The word held a tiny inflection, a hint of criticism that he'd come on such ceremony.

The last delegation from the Indus, and even before that from Kemet, had both been simple, small affairs that Aurelia had easily commandeered and reduced to something a little less formal than the signatories had expected. Here, with Aulus's deputies and underlings all garbed in formal regalia, Aurelia was no doubt uncomfortable as for all intents and purposes, with his weapons and show of might, he'd established himself as the stronger of the two.

Not the best foot to put forward, Max thought. But then he'd grown to know Aurelia very well in the passing years. Now he was on tenterhooks, waiting to find out what Mara had hinted would possibly upset the Commander.

Aulus was bowing, paying his respects to Aurelia. "My colleagues and staff wished to be here too, to pay their respects."

Aurelia smiled and waved a hand to the members of her personal guard who stood around the room. Stationed at intervals and bearing long-staffed spears, they were not present merely for decoration. Each and every one of them were skilled swordsmen and women, and fighters.

The two who guarded the door opened it in a flourish, and Mara bent to speak in Aulus's ear. Whatever she said to the man, it sent the blood rushing to his face. His skin darkened to nearly black, and his eyes widened. His jaw pulsed as he appeared to struggle with something. After a few moments, he turned to his second in command, and spoke a word in his ear.

The 2IC as well seemed surprised, but he stood to his feet, tucked his helmet under his arm and walked off. Though he didn't give any signal that Max could see, the rest of the contingent got to their feet and followed the man out.

Max wasn't sure whose power he admired more now, that of Aulus or of Aurelia the Oracle of Pythia.

Aulus watched his men leave and only when the door had shut behind them did he shift his attention to the old seer. "I apologize if I acted without forethought."

Mara cackled. "The previous liaison to the Pythia knew full well what her preferences are. She does not like the pomp and circumstance that comes with large delegations such as this one."

Aulus had the grace to bow his head instead of responding with what he was thinking. Max was certain from the flash of anger he'd seen in the man's eyes, that he'd not appreciated the dismissal of his team. But, Max had to hope he'd appreciate that their removal had been done tactfully and without antagonism.

Aurelia was waving Mara off, bringing Max's attention back to the conversation. "I am concerned though, Commander Aulus," she said, her tone devoid of emotion. "I had requested the opportunity to choose a specific person to liaise with. But it seems my request was denied. And I wasn't informed of that denial."

Aulus shook his head and frowned, but Max detected a tightening in the man's features. "Again, I must apologize. I fear it must be a miscommunication as I was not informed of this request. I'm afraid everything had been put in place already with regard to my attachment as liaison."

Aurelia tilted her head. "My dear young man. Are you saying that I have no choice in the matter? Because if you are, then I have to admit I would be quite taken aback. Every other country in the world allows me to have some input in the decision as to who their delegate will be. I am, after all, the person who can see into the future. It has always been a requirement, Commander Aulus. And I am more than disappointed that my request has been dismissed like the wishes of a foolish old woman would be." Aurelia's voice had risen, and with every octave she scaled, Aulus grew more uncomfortable.

She paused as though she was taking a breath, but Aulus replied, "I must sincerely apologize, my Lady. I will return immediately and investigate your request. We will ensure we find someone who you feel is more suited to the role." Aulus's voice was tight, and hard. The sound of a man deeply offended and whose ire was steadily rising.

"Oh calm yourself, dear boy. What's done is done. I will not allow you to lose face by leaving me only to have a replacement sent out in your stead. I will agree to a one-year period in which you will groom the person I have chosen to be your liaison."

Aulus's eyebrows rose. It was clear the man didn't feel Aurelia bore the right to make such a choice, but short of causing an international incident, the commander had little choice but to comply. No doubt he'd return to his superiors and attempt to overturn Aurelia's decree.

He cleared his throat and hesitated. "Very well, my Lady. Thank you for ensuring I do not lose face with my peers or my superiors."

The old seer nodded and then clapped her hands together.

"I'm so glad you agree because I wish for you to assist me with my selected liaison."

The commander smiled though his mouth was a thin line that lacked any cheer. "May I ask who your choice of replacement is?"

Aurelia nodded. "Of course," she said, waving a hand and turning to say, "Meet Max Vissarion."

CHAPTER 9

*M*ax had drawn the attention of many a soldier within the military too.

Aulus hadn't been ecstatic at Max's appointment to what Aulus had considered a prime role, but Max's work ethic, his talent as a soldier and his dedication to Aurelia had impressed the commander. Aulus had reluctantly mentored Max once he'd seen that the younger man was hard-working. It seemed that a strong work-ethic had been the key to gaining the commander's support.

Max had trained hard and sailed through military school, entering the army officially at the age of nineteen when his role of liaison had become official. He'd been shipped off to distant war zones with a caveat that should the Pythia call he'd be flown directly to her.

Max had felt guilty for leaving her, even though he knew Mara was fully capable of translation for Aurelia. But Max had grown fond of the crotchety old woman.

On his first tour, he'd been attached to a platoon of Tirones; new recruits who would train for anything from three to twelve months before transition to the next level. Both men and women were provided with equal access to the army, though there were still a few politicians who believed a woman's place was at home. From what Max saw on his first day in formal service, he had to disagree.

His commander, Bridgette Gordia, was tough as nails, and harder on her recruits than even old Codimus had been. She'd put the team through their paces on the first day, ordering a barefooted run over hills littered with sharp stones, shrapnel, and shards of glass.

Max, whose soles had been calloused with running through the Argentinean hillside, had run the course with ease. He'd completed his run and had barely broken a sweat, and was picking a short piece of metal from his heel when a shout went up from the middle of the obstacle course. One of the recruits was trying to lift what looked like the barrel of a half-exploded cannon. Max frowned as he stared at the boy, whose shock of dreadlocks shivered around his head, his muscles bulging as he strained to lift the weapon.

A shout of laughter went up, and a fellow recruit slapped his thigh. "Look at that. How chivalrous of him to help the helpless female." The boy grunted as his companion elbowed him hard in the gut and jerked his chin at the commander who stood not ten feet from him.

Though silenced, the kid continued to smile widely as Dread-locks strained to move the cannon. From Max's location, he was able to see that the cannon had fallen and trapped another recruit whose blonde ponytail shone like gold. He couldn't see her face, but despite the awkward angle of the cannon, she didn't seem to be in pain.

Max shouldered past a small cluster of recruits, noticing that not one of them seemed inclined to offer assistance. True, the test of the course had been to get through first or at least to be among the top ten percent. Failing hadn't been an option and as Max watched he realized that Dreadlocks had forgotten the race entirely and was focused on helping the girl.

Max gritted his teeth and threw caution to the wind. Sure, he wanted to come out on top, but not at the risk of someone's health or mortality being on the line. He surged past the front line and raced onto the field, easily avoiding the many obstacles on his path.

He reached the boy whose brown skin glistened with perspiration. He glanced up, bright golden-brown eyes wide with frustration.

He hesitated as he stared at Max, who nodded at him and glanced down at the girl. "The cannon slipped in the mud. Couple of kids jumped it before Les did and it slid just as she got to it."

The girl groaned. "It's not anyone's fault. I should have been paying attention. Should have gone around instead of trying to show off." She let out a sigh. "Fuck, I hate being the damsel in distress."

"Then why don't you do something about it?" asked Max.

The girl—Les—frowned as she studied his face. "You got a plan buddy? Do tell cos I'm all outta options over here."

"Study your surroundings, assess your position, decide on the most logical course of action." Max jerked a chin at a thin metal rod that sat beside Les's head. "Won't know if it will help unless you try." He wanted to tell her more, but he'd already sensed the presence of commander Gordia behind him, and he wanted the girl to succeed on her own. Even if she failed the course, she'd earn herself some credit for getting out of her situation using her own head.

The girl's eyes narrowed, and Max paused.

Had he misjudged her?

CHAPTER 10

*S*he seemed to consider his words for a moment. She glanced over at the cannon, then at how it lay across her body, where its end sat on a shallow rock at her side. She was fixed in place by the position and weight of the cannon, but there was a way out.

Max realized she was squinting more because he had the sun at his back and it was unlikely she'd be able to see more than just his outline.

Then she grinned and reached for the rod, sliding it toward her with her fingers until she could grab a hold of it. She gripped it firmly then angled it beneath her torso, slowly digging and scraping away the mud from beneath her back. It had felt like an excruciatingly long time, but from what Max had assessed, it had been a simple thing. The cannon was weighing her down but only to a certain extent. All she'd needed to do was to lower herself out from beneath it, and the soft muddy soil was easy enough to remove with a small implement.

At last, she shimmied out from beneath the cannon and boosted to her feet. "Thanks for…" she paused her gaze flickering momentarily over Max's shoulder, "...the belief in me." She nodded, her cheeks still red from the effort.

Then Max and Dreadlocks—who had been exceptionally quiet—came face-to-face with Gordia whose lips had formed a thin tight line.

"Vissarion? Assante?" she addressed Max and Dreadlocks. "I don't believe you are required to lurk while a fellow recruit is attempting to complete the course."

Assante paused and looked over at Max. "It's my fault, Commander. I stopped to help, and he came to assist."

Gordia peered around the two boys and studied Les. Max would have killed to have seen the girl's expression. Then the commander said, "I don't see how she needed your help. I respect your chivalry—"

"It wasn't chivalry, commander."

Gordia looked over at Max, and her eyes narrowed. She was a tall, imposing woman, her frame slim and muscled. Her pale hair was braided into a bun at the back of her head, and she exuded power, and oddly a sense of safety. "Explain yourself, Tiro."

Max gave a shallow bow. "I apologize, commander. What I meant was I would have assisted no matter the sex of my fallen comrade. From where I'd stood, I couldn't tell that Tiro was a female, so I'd given no special treatment to her gender."

Gordia's lip curled slightly at the corner before she straightened and gave a sharp nod. She shifted a cool regard to Assante, who, despite the deeper brown of his skin was clearly going red —and said, "I assume you too suffered from the same affliction of offering your comrades assistance regardless of sex."

Assante hesitated and glanced over at Max who glared at him hard.

The boy cleared his throat. "I'm afraid so, Commander," he said straightening his spine.

The commander nodded and walked around the two before she stood before Les. "There was a man once, centuries ago who had said something like 'give a man a fish, and you will feed him today, but teach a man to fish, and you will feed him for the rest of his life.' Do you understand what I mean Tiro Avesta?"

The girl nodded. "Saving a person from a dangerous situation is one thing but teaching that person the tools with which to free themselves will save them multiple times over in their future lives."

Gordia smiled and nodded. "Well learned, Tiro. Now you and your comrades may leave the field. We will begin the next challenge shortly."

The trio didn't wait to be told again. They marched back to the waiting group of recruits and took their positions in the lines as the commander returned from the field.

The rest of the month passed uneventfully, with Gordia putting all of the recruits through a grueling pace that had at least a dozen pull out of their own accord, and which had failed more than twenty. Not everyone was cut out for the army, and it was clear from the variety of recruits that had arrived on the first day.

But Assante—whose first name Max soon discovered was Marcus—and Avesta, had remained as strong and as resilient as Max himself and had passed each of the minor levels with flying colors. When Max had progressed to Miles within two months, he'd worried that leaving the two behind would affect their fast-formed friendship.

But thankfully, despite their continued differences in rank as the three progressed over the twelve-month training, they remained friends, and had even taken to boarding in the same lodge. His friendship with Celestra Avesta had grown too, from friendly rivalry to blossoming affection.

Max had fallen into a routine, training, studying, downtime with his new friends.

Until Max was called away to see Aurelia.

CHAPTER 11

A helicopter arrived for Max during one of their training sessions. It had been the first urgent call in the twelve months since he'd entered the military and Max had progressed from Miles to Decanus and been placed in charge of a group of eight milites which had included both Marcus and Les.

They'd just entered their barracks after a long day of training when a messenger stormed into their galley and yelled for Max.

"Vissarion! You're to come to the airfield, Site 3 H for immediate takeoff." The messenger yelled then turned on his heel and fled.

Marcus, who had been lifting a forkful of peas to his mouth, paused and frowned. Looking over at Max he said, "So if you weren't here to hear him, guess you'd miss the chopper?"

Max grunted and pushed aside his plate of boiled corn, peas and bland strips of what appeared to be chicken but tasted like feet. "Sorry, milites. I have to go. I should return in a day or so."

He got to his feet and hurried away, not lingering to explain where he was going or why. He'd not revealed his role with the Pythia to either Marcus or Les, and he was worried it would set him further apart from them than he'd already been placed. His role as Decanus, being put in charge of his friends, had made him tense and worried that perhaps one day their relationships would crumble because one or both of them would not be comfortable working under his authority.

Until now, that hadn't happened, but Max suspected that once he revealed his position as NGS Liaison to the Pythia, his friends might see him in a different light.

The helicopter took him to an airfield near the training ground, and Max caught a small plane over to Argentina. They stopped to refuel twice which annoyed Max and amped up the anxious feeling he had building inside his gut. If the Pythia needed him urgently, the hours wasted on traveling to see her, could likely amount to a dangerous waste of time.

Max had slept in fits and starts, and had risen from his seat long before the pilot had given the okay for him to stand. As soon as the door opened, he was hurrying down the steps and into the car that was waiting for him, engine running.

MAX ENTERED Aurelia's private room, searching out the hunched form of the oracle as she reclined on the seat beside the window. The sun was low, and the rays lit her hair, turning them into strands of gold. When she looked up at Max, he paused at the sight of her pale eyes.

"Are you well, my Lady?" he asked softly, going to her side.

She waved him off. "I am fine. But you need to hurry."

"What is it?" Her tone worried him, saying that whatever she was about to reveal was terribly urgent.

"A cruise liner in the Mediterranean is going to sink. All eight hundred and twenty passengers and crew will die."

Max stiffened. "How will I stop them from sailing?"

Aurelia shrugged. "Sink the boat before it leaves? Raise an inquiry? Pull their licenses? I don't know." Aurelia tossed her hands in the air and got to her feet. She was muttering something to herself, then turned to Max. "Mara will send someone with you. I'd much prefer you have some protection just in case."

Max laughed. "I don't need protection. I'm sure I can do this alone. You need not trouble your warriors. Besides, don't I have a magic boar to look after me?"

The old woman lifted her rheumy eyes in Max's direction. "You don't understand, do you. Xales will protect you, but only to a certain extent."

"Certain extent?"

Aurelia nodded. "Xales's main role is the protection of the Pythia. Given a choice he'd choose to save her life over that of the Immunis." She shrugged. "He will perform his core duty."

Frowning, Max shook his head. "I'm not sure what you mean."

"There is one more responsibility of the Immunis, my boy. But don't worry. This does not apply to me. I believe I'm a little too old for you." The old woman let out a soft chuckle. Max's brow furrowed as she continued to speak. "Through the ages, the Oracle's Immunis—especially because he is immune to her prophetic touch—has served as more than translator. More than just companion."

She smiled, her lips curling into a smirk.

"The Immunis will also be husband to his Pythia."

MAX GRITTED his teeth as he settled into the seat, strapping himself in for takeoff. He'd left Aurelia, filled with anger at her words, at what she'd held back from him.

He remembered his anger, and her attempts at making him understand. What did he need to understand? That he was destined to be the husband of the next Pythia?

What crazy nonsense was the old woman trying to sell him? She'd convinced him that he was this Immunis, the translator to the Pythias, but to be the destined mate of an oracle he had yet to meet?

It was preposterous in the extreme and Max was not about to bow to the prophecy, or to the oracle who spoke it.

His last words to her had been filled with anger and disappointment. He'd promised to continue to help Aurelia because he believed in the oracle and her duty to the people of the world. He'd even assured her that he would remain loyal to the next oracle after Aurelia transferred her powers. But his last words to her had been spoken from the heart.

"Nobody tells me who I'm supposed to marry. And nobody tells me who I'm supposed to love."

CHAPTER 12

The flight to Marukash was bumpy and uncomfortable and far too long. When Max arrived, still in the crumpled pants and shirt he'd worn on arrival in Argentina, he was greeted by a wave of suffocating heat. Mara had advised Max that the Moroccan liaison to the Pythia had been notified of the urgency of the situation and would arrange a car for him.

True to their word, a dusty old Hatcher 62 was waiting for him as he descended the stairs. There was no checking of passports either, just a wave at him to jump into the open-backed, roofless vehicle. Max obeyed, no time to waste as he considered his options.

Sink the ship before it left the dock. He liked that idea simply because—from what Mara had expanded on as she'd accompanied him to the plane—the ship-owners were aware of the issue with the engine. Some sort of malfunction of the portside engines that would result in an explosion mid-sea.

Why not find a way to trigger that explosion before the vessel departed, before staff and passengers arrived onboard? Max's single attempt at conversation with his blue-turbaned driver had been met with a shake of the head and a wobbly wave which he'd interpreted as the man was unable to speak to him.

Max waited until he was dropped off at the NGS embassy where a thin, tall man was waiting at reception, pacing a narrow stretch of carpet.

"Greetings, you must be Max Vissarion?" the man reached for Max's hand and shook it vigorously. "I'm Giran Solam. I've spoken to Mara, and I'm here to confirm I'm at your service. The Moroccan council of Elders are aware of the dangers and are offering you every assistance no matter the requirement. The ship-owners have license to dock here but should we revoke that license we risk them sailing out to open water and still transporting passengers onboard."

Max nodded. Giran had answered most of the questions that had been spinning around in Max's head. "Do you have a submersible?"

Giran smiled and nodded. "We have a fully functional prototype. How deep and how far will you need it to go?"

Max smiled. "Not far at all. I just need to get near enough to the ship that should I have to jump over the edge, I'll have it close by. Close enough for me to get inside before the explosion."

Giran nodded, his expression thoughtful and somewhat impressed. "I'd come with you, but I'm unfortunately not skilled in such tactical warfare."

Laughing, Max said, "Neither am I. I'm just fulfilling my orders." Giran motioned for Max to follow, then began to walk to the entrance of the hotel.

"I'll need schematics for the vessel, and I'll need you to make a call for me too. Get someone else to do it. Whatever works best. But you need to make a call to dock security. Something that will have the cruise liner pull away from the dock. I'd prefer the vessel as far away from the landing as possible to limit damage from the explosion."

Giran drummed his fingers on his thigh. "How will an evacuation of heavier vessels sound? Maybe because water levels in the port area will be dropping due to an issue with the locks?"

Max was impressed at the man's ingenuity. "Can you pull it off?"

"Absolutely. It doesn't have to be true. Just needs to *sound* true."

CHAPTER 13

*G*iran headed to the very same Hatcher, and Max jumped in.

"I'll drop you off at one of the export facilities on the east dock. It's two berths away from the cruise liner in question—The Principessa. I'll have the submersible delivered to the closest dock, along with the explosives."

With that the man braked and rolled to a stop in front of a darkened warehouse facility, a dusty sign proclaiming Honoria Export Goods.

Max jumped off as the man slowed, barely clearing the vehicle before he took off. With the darkness falling over the city, all Max could see of the vehicle were two pale orange brake lights. He hoped Giran would hold up his end of the plan, but Max had to focus on his part.

He hurried closer to the entrance, ducking behind a stack of barrels marked with Honoria's initials. An hour later, a small truck swayed into view and came to a stop near the water's edge. It backed up against the ramp, and the driver alighted, rounding the vehicle to unhook something large and metallic. A low grinding echoed across the way as the submersible slipped into the water.

Then the driver calmly closed the back of his truck and jumped back inside, driving off without a glance backward.

Max was up.

He scurried across the wide road, using the boxes and crates scattered randomly along the way to hide his progress. The dark night only served to aid him, and before long he was sliding into the submersible, and guiding it quickly underwater and out of sight.

Inside the small space, Max found the explosives fitted inside a wide bag no bigger than the purse Les carried when she wanted to get all dressed up and feminine. Giran had obtained a full body wetsuit as well, complete with face mask and mini double oxygen tank, as well as the ship's schematics protected by a thin envelope of plastic.

Giran had thought well ahead of Max. Either that or diving gear was standard issue with a submersible.

Max changed into the diving gear, looped the explosives over his shoulders and guided the sub out toward the edge of the pier. From there he waited, watching the sonar as the minutes ticked by. Forty minutes later, he detected movement as The Principessa began to back away from the dock. Max had to wait only a little longer, before gliding out beside the ship and closing in near where the schematics had indicated the engine would be.

Max attached the sub to the ship using the giant suction pads on the side of the sub. Even though the ship was still moving, Max exited the sub and climbed up the side of the ship using metal handholds carved into the vessel's body. At the top, he jumped lightly onto the deck and hurried to the nearest door. Inside he turned left then right, then took the stairs down two flights.

Max moved fast, setting the charges around the engine. He knew it would have been far better to mess with the engine itself, but he hadn't had sufficient time to find a ship's engineer who would be willing and able to help him. He was a foreign element, easy for him to disappear without a trace. Not so easy for the likes of Giran and his contacts.

Work done, Max set the timers and turned to leave, and walked straight into a large, barrel-chested man wearing blue oil-stained overalls.

Well, Max had asked for a ship's engineer after all. Brought new meaning to the phrase be careful what you wish for.

CHAPTER 14

*M*ax ducked in time to avoid a left hook, then slammed his heel into the enormous man's knee. Max felt the bone shatter beneath his heel and weaved to avoid a second punch, one that had the power of pain and fury behind it.

Max ducked another punch and landed one of his own upward to the man's chin, glancing at the timers on the explosives.

Three minutes.

He had no time to waste with this brute, but he couldn't risk the man following him out of the engine room or raising an alarm. The punch to the jaw had done some damage and blood streamed from the man's mouth.

Max charged, slamming his full weight into the man's torso then jabbed him twice in the throat as his momentum shoved the man into a railing. The engineer flailed backward, and Max stepped away allowing the man's weight and momentum to pull him over the railing.

Max didn't wait to confirm the man's demise. Instead, he ran for the door, snicking it open to check the hall. Racing for the stairs he climbed them fast, moving on his toes. Marcus would be impressed at Max's grace.

Reaching the outer door, Max heard a shout from behind him. Throwing all caution to the wind, he raced for the edge and dove over and straight into the water, praying all the way down that he'd judge correctly as to where the sub was.

Thankfully, he didn't dive right into it and flatten his brain as he'd imagined. Instead, he entered the water two feet from the sub, and dived beneath it to hide his movements. He unhooked the suction cups using the exterior manual levers then guided the sub down and away from the ship. Above him, the security scanned the water with spotlights as Max counted down another minute.

Two minutes to go.

Underwater now, he had no way of entering the sub again until he was certain he wouldn't be seen. He had no choice but to swim, and guided the sub back to the dock outside Honoria's. It felt like ages had passed, and Max was tapping out the last of oxygen tank one, and just switched to tank two when he rounded the dock and came to the surface.

Sucking in deep breaths, Max guided the sub to the edge of the dock then submerged it two feet beneath the water. He kept the black wetsuit on and emerged from the water, another shadow to add to the night. Weaving between the crates and boxes, Max landed behind the barrels only to hear the sound of booted feet hitting the ground.

With nowhere to hide, the door to the office behind him tightly locked, Max had no choice but to try the lid of one of the barrels.

He gagged and dragged on the oxygen mask and dived into the barrel full of fermented seafood. Probably destined for some far-off town where fermented sea slugs were a delicacy that probably aided in one's virility.

Max submerged himself within the barrel's contents and waited as what sounded like a small team searched the area.

They'd almost reached Max, when an explosion rocked the dock eliciting yells from the men who had been tossed to the ground. Someone backed into Max's barrel, and it tipped over spilling the foul-smelling muck onto the ground, the lip rolling away and hitting the door to the store.

Voices echoed, and Max froze as shadows swayed back and forth. Then after what felt like ages, the team retreated, probably called back to deal with the aftermath of the explosion.

It felt like another age until Giran arrived to retrieved Max.

Max was not amused when the man insisted that Max remained inside the barrel and proceeded to seal it securely. Max was forced to travel all the way to the embassy, and be transported through the kitchen and into an interior washroom before he was allowed to get out.

As he peeled off the wetsuit, he wrinkled his nose.

Cerberus' balls! This stench was going to take forever to get rid of.

CHAPTER 15

$\mathcal{M}$ax had had a hard time living down the taint of the rotten sea slugs.

The odor hung around him for more than a week, and no amount of bathing helped. Celestra had taken to lighting sticks of incense around the barracks and Max had had to suffer his milites turning their noses up at him even when he was handing out orders. He'd seen the comedy in it, but hadn't shown his amusement to his infantrymen.

Marcus and Les though, had enjoyed poking fun at him, and had only agreed to sit at the same table with him for dinner when the stench had faded.

Les's amusement had brightened her blue eyes, making them twinkle. And Max thought back to Aurelia's edicts. Max was twenty and ready to transition to a non-service position.

And when Aulus had visited to offer Max a place in his newly formed division at the NGS, Max was hard put to refuse the offer.

"You can continue to be liaison to the Pythia for as long as she will have you," Aulus had said, dangling a carrot Max could not ignore. The man had come down to the barracks and had sequestered Max in his private office, a small space, but one that befitted his rank as Decanus.

Aulus stood at the window, his back to the night, his dark face brightened by the overhead light. "How long do you need to make your decision?" Aulus asked.

"I don't know what the position is yet sir. Will there be a debriefing?"

Aulus reached out, turning his hand over to reveal a scroll wound around a wooden rod. Each end bore a carving of the standard of the NGS, confirming it as an official document.

Max cracked the red wax seal and rolled the scroll open, reading as he went. "FAPA?"

"Federal Agency for Paranormal Affairs. It's a specialized branch of the Federal Investigative Services."

Max didn't need to ask what it specialized in. Its unimaginative name gave it away. "Why me?" he asked softly. "I have skills to offer my country."

"But your position as Liaison supersedes all other roles. Until the Pythia is of the mind to set you aside, you are permanently attached to her on behalf of the country." Max could have sworn he'd heard a hint of bitterness in Aulus's voice, but when he looked up at the commander's face, he saw no sign of emotion.

"Oh, and the position at FAPA requires a tertiary education." Max opened his mouth to name his military school honors, but Aulus cut him off. "I'm well aware of your academic performance, but unfortunately this is a requirement for entry to the FAPA head office. You'll be my second in command and will take the position of commander when I move into the more senior general role."

Max noted the man's ambition and was tempted to question him on his timeframe. But he bit his tongue and maintained the respect that Aulus's position demanded.

Max stared at the papers, thinking of what life would be like outside of the military. Then he looked up at Aulus, making the decision on instinct. "Am I able to make a request, sir?"

Aulus paused, half turned to make for the door. "Go ahead."

Max took a breath. "Could I request two milites to be invited as well?"

Aulus smiled. "Commander Gordia had already apprised us of the tightly-knit unit you three make. They've been invited as well."

"And the university?"

"That too."

"Thank you, sir."

"Don't thank me. Show me I'm not making a mistake."

UNIVERSITY LIFE PROCEEDED in a fashion that made Max grateful that classes were nightly and that he could be useful working at the FAPA head office during the day. Marcus had often complained that normal humans needed sleep, but he'd kept up anyway.

Two years passed before Max found himself living with Les and contemplating the big question.

"Do you really think you two are meant for each other?" Marcus asked as Max dropped a box onto the desk in his new office. He'd been moved to Interim Commander, a position that would last a year or two before Aulus designated Max full Commander of FAPA head office.

Max pulled out the plaque that his parents had made for him, a Latin saying that equated one's parents to gods. It had been a joke, but Max had appreciated it more than they had realized. Now it sat atop a sideboard beside his many awards and medals. And beside the gift from Aurelia—a brass statue of a wide-eyed boar with a gold ring through its nose.

"He looks dangerous," said Marcus, eyeing the statue.

"He is," Max replied without thinking. But when he looked up to cover up his faux pas, Marcus had already left and was walking out to his desk.

Marcus's words rang in his head though. Did he really love Les? Max cared for her deeply, which he knew meant he loved her. Had Aurelia succeeded in confusing him enough that he'd not trust his own heart?

CHAPTER 16

*I*n the end, he hadn't proposed to Les.

Their fighting only increased in frequency until Max was beginning to question why they were still together. One night, he'd just reached the apartment he shared with Les and had stuck a fork into a juicy steak when his phone began to ring. Les glared at him, but Max had had little choice.

"I have to answer, Les. As Interim Commander if I put one foot wrong, I could lose everything. If we want a better place to live in, I can't risk being careless." He'd used his FAPA position as a reason to answer, but they both knew who the call was from.

Les sat back and raised her wine goblet to her lips. Better she drank than to argue with him. When he cut the call, her face had darkened. "I know that look. You have to go?"

Max cut a fat portion of the steak and stuck it in his mouth. As he chewed, he said, "I have to go. It's what being Liaison entails."

Les snorted and reached for the bottle of cabernet sauvignon, his father's aged line. "All it does is make you her bitch."

Max swallowed hard and got to his feet so fast that his chair toppled over. Les's eyes widened for the briefest moment and then she lowered her lids and concentrated on drinking.

Max left her there to simmer and headed into the bath. He showered and changed, then packed a set of clothes as well as a uniform. There were times when he never knew what he was heading into when Aurelia called.

He walked into the dining room to find Les pouring the last of the bottle of wine into her glass. Her eyes were glazed, but she gritted her jaw tight, the tension emanating from her body like a wave.

"I wish you would understand, Les. This is something that's important to me. You've known that since forever."

"I never realized how much she controlled you."

"It's not about control. It's about duty. The desire to do something good for the world."

Les snorted. "For what? For politicians to ensure they maintain control? For corporations to eliminate competition?" There was a cold edge to her voice that Max didn't like. No, the iciness hurt him deeply.

"I don't know why you can't support me on this. Yes, I'm called out at a moment's notice. I was going to..." Max realized how close he was to confessing he'd been waiting for the right moment to pop the question. Then he cleared his throat. "I think we need some time apart. When I return, I'll stay with Marcus for a few days. Maybe we need to...think."

Les got to her feet, her face crumpling as she began to sob. Max ignored her and kept walking. At the door, he paused to look back at her. "You selfish bastard! You're making a goddamn choice, you know that?"

Max sighed, the pain something more than he could bear. He opened the door and shut it just in time.

Glass crashed into the door, and he heard Les scream out, "You'll leave me for her?"

Beneath a shroud of sadness, Max left the building and

headed out to the waiting car. He'd go to Aurelia and deal with whatever she wanted.

Then he had to think about his future, because he was no longer sure that being the Liaison to the Pythia was good for him.

Or for Les.

CHAPTER 17

*M*ax wasn't sure what to think of Aurelia's prediction.

"An oil refinery in the Eastern Slavic States, is going to explode. Some kind of system malfunction. But the pipelines to and from the refinery were built beneath the surrounding towns. Any explosion is going to have a flow-on effect along the pipes themselves. We know from the schematics report that the pipes are vented at various locations which from what we've been able to ascertain, will guarantee total obliteration of everything within a two-mile radius, as well as extensive damage and radiation poisoning at least eight miles out. We're also looking at the toxic pollution of rivers and water tables as well as evaporation and rainfall. We're talking acid rain."

Max was addressing Aulus, at the request of Aurelia who'd stressed how bad the situation could get.

"Their army won't let us anywhere near that refinery."

"Even if we tell them what we know?"

Aulus shook his head. "Those people are Extreme Stalinists but with a twisted agenda. Even if we offer help, they will turn us down, out of pride or suspicion, it doesn't matter."

"So what are we talking? Covert op?"

Aulus nodded as he tapped his charcoal pencil on his desk. "Gather a recon team. We have two black sites in the area. This will have to be off the books, so we don't ruffle certain feathers."

Max hated when things leaned toward diplomacy. It usually meant his hands were tied. Which was what he didn't need on this particular op. He nodded and exhaled. "I'll get the team together. We leave in four hours."

"That soon?"

"Aurelia wasn't able to give me a specific timeframe. She couldn't see anything that would help date the event, which means we have to treat it as an imminent threat."

Aulus nodded, his expression confirming that he was satisfied with Max's conclusions. "Let me know when you're ready. I'll arrange a plane now. You're going trans-pacific, so you'll have rough weather and turbulence most of the way. You going to manage the bumpy flight?"

Max nodded. He didn't realize that Aulus knew of his issue with flying. Ever since he'd returned from Marukash, he'd suffered from terrible nausea on every flight. Les had teased him saying he was the only person on the planet who suffered from PTSD from overexposure to intense odor.

She may well have been right.

Aulus cleared his throat. "There are places—"

"Marcus has a list for me. I've been taking a few things. I'll figure it out eventually."

Aulus nodded, and Max wondered if the man was enjoying what was clearly a failure on Max's part. But Aulus merely tapped his pencil again.

Max left soon after and selected the team, debriefing them swiftly and making it clear they were going dark and that they could possibly not return. There were many somber faces around the team, but none chose to remain behind even when Max offered that as an option with no judgment or consequences.

Max had considered calling Celestra, going home and talking with her. But with the limited time, and with wheels up in under an hour, he had little choice in the matter.

Marcus had insisted on joining the team, claiming that Aulus needed to stretch his muscles every now and again. And that the rest of the team would manage just fine.

Max hoped he was right.

But even as the plane took off, with his team all strapped in and ready, Max felt something strange twist in his gut. And it had nothing to do with nausea.

He usually went with his gut. And today his gut was telling him that something was wrong.

CHAPTER 18

*M*ax and the team moved like shadows down a long catwalk that overlooked the portion of the refinery that Aurelia had claimed was where the explosions had originated.

When the team reached the location, Max was horrified to find that the pressure had passed the danger level. The team studied the schematics and scanned the room. Up above them on the left wall was an office that overlooked the control room. Max sent two of his team up to check the room, then sent two more out of the main hall to investigate why the place was empty.

Before the two even reached the door, Max heard Marcus's voice on the overhead speaker system. "We have to get the hell out of here. This thing's gonna blow. The facility was evacuated thirty minutes ago."

There was a short pause while Max wondered how long they had.

The speaker screeched, and Marcus's voice echoed around the team. "T minus twenty minutes and three seconds."

Before he could say the word, the entire team turned as one

and began to evacuate. Marcus and his partner rappelled back down to the ground floor and brought up the rear.

"Aurelia was right to say we needed to move now," muttered Max as they raced along the corridors. Red lights flashed, and alarms rang announcing the countdown to detonation.

"Something went wrong inside there, Max. It wasn't an accident. They did something deliberately, or maybe pushed things too far."

"And they managed to evacuate early enough to get out of the danger zone."

"Did they evacuate the towns?"

"Not that I saw. There were no public announcements or even a notice to the nearby towns to flee the blast radius."

Max's jaw hurt at the thought that the bastards had left thousands of innocent people to die.

The team burst into the daylight out of the tunnel entrance, but not one of them paused to take a breath. They ran for the hillside and scrambled up the steep incline, racing for the two black bullet-proof army issue four-wheel-drives. Tires skidded, and doors slammed, and the vehicles took off. All heads turned to watch through the back windows.

Behind them the explosion rocked the refinery, the blast sending a gigantic ball of flame into the air. Vibrations rippled along the ground and through the air, lifting both vehicles off the ground at least two yards before dropping them back down.

Neither vehicle slowed even though they skidded as their tires hit solid ground. They drove along the back of a small village where the vented pipelines spewed fire and gas into the air. Clouds of poisonous smoke covered the town. The screams of the villagers echoed through the air, and out of the darkness, a figure came running.

Flames covered the boy and Max acted out of instinct, without a thought to his own safety. He shoved open the door and flung himself out, landing on the ground and rolling over into a crouch. He raced for the child, throwing the boy onto the ground and rolling him in the dirt to put out the flames. Max's palms stung from where he'd been forced to touch the child, but he didn't pay any attention to the pain.

Tires skidded behind Max, and someone held out an emergency foil blanket. It was a new introduction into their first aid kits, apparently appropriate whether to keep a person warm or cool them down depending on which side you used. Max chose the cool side and wrapped the blanket around the boy.

Even as they carried him to the car, Max heard the wheezing of the child's lungs, and his gut tightened.

They kept driving, and Max watched the boy the entire time, feeding him water with a straw, injecting him with painkillers and antibiotics and praying to Apollo that the boy would survive.

The fallout of the blast was nothing like Max had ever expected. The Union of United Nations came down hard on the government of the small Slavic state, placed sanctions on them and removed various trade rights.

The world mourned for the dead and the dying, and for those within the path of the poisonous cloud that had traveled away from the blast site. Across the world, governments had specialists testing constantly to ensure they knew when and where the cloud would reach them. Two years later they were still waiting and watching.

The little boy lasted twenty hours before succumbing to lung failure. He'd had little chance of survival, and though Max had cursed Apollo, he'd have to have expected the god to work miracles.

And the gods were not known for granting miracles.

Les had come by to see Marcus and Max, claiming that she needed to see if they were both doing okay. She'd cleaned and cooked while they slept and relaxed, regained their physical strength. But when Max and Marcus looked into each other's faces, they relived the horror of the awful night.

Max had listened quietly when Les had apologized for her horrible words, then she'd explained that she understood now why he needed to work with Aurelia, that she wanted to fix their relationship. But there'd been something broken between them for a long time, and Max had finally gained the strength to admit it to himself.

When Max had told Les that he was done, that he could no longer pursue their relationship, and that it was too late for them as a couple, she didn't explode or rant and rave. She didn't get angry. She just looked at him sadly and then kissed him on the cheek.

She wished him well and walked out of the door and out of his life.

There had been no way to fix what had been broken.

Max worked purely on trust.

~ TO BE CONTINUED ~

Thank you for reading. The DARK SIGHT Series continues with SHADOW SIGHT.

FREE STARTER LIBRARY - JOIN MY NEWSLETTER

Get the following titles FREE when you subscribe to my newsletter.

Tee's Newsletter

http://smarturl.it/TeesMailingList

ABOUT THE AUTHOR

I have been a writer from the time I was old enough to recognize that reading was a doorway into my imagination. Poetry was my first foray into the art of the written word. Books were my best friends, my escape, my haven. I am essentially a recluse but this part of my personality is impossible to practice given I have two teenage daughters, who are actually my friends, my tea-makers, my confidantes… I am blessed with a husband who has left me for golf. It's a fair trade as I have left him for writing. We are both passionate supporters of each other's loves – it works wonderfully…

My heart is currently broken in two. One half resides in South Africa where my old roots still remain, and my heart still longs for the endless beaches and the smell of moist soil after a summer downpour. My love for Ma Afrika will never fade. The other half of me has been transplanted to the Land of the Long White Cloud. The land of the Taniwha, beautiful Maraes, and volcanoes. The land of green, pure beauty that truly inspires. And because I am so torn between these two lands – I shall forever remain cross-eyed.

Stalk Tee here:
www.tgayer.com
tee@tgayer.com

facebook.com/TGAyerAuthor

twitter.com/TGAyerAuthor

bookbub.com/profile/t-g-ayer